My father
always works
with his hands.

He builds
things in his
workshop.

He measures
with his ruler,
marking the wood
with a pencil. Then
he measures again,
just to be sure.

He's picky.
When I help, I try to
do things like he does.
He's showing me how
to paint, pound nails
straight, and saw wood.

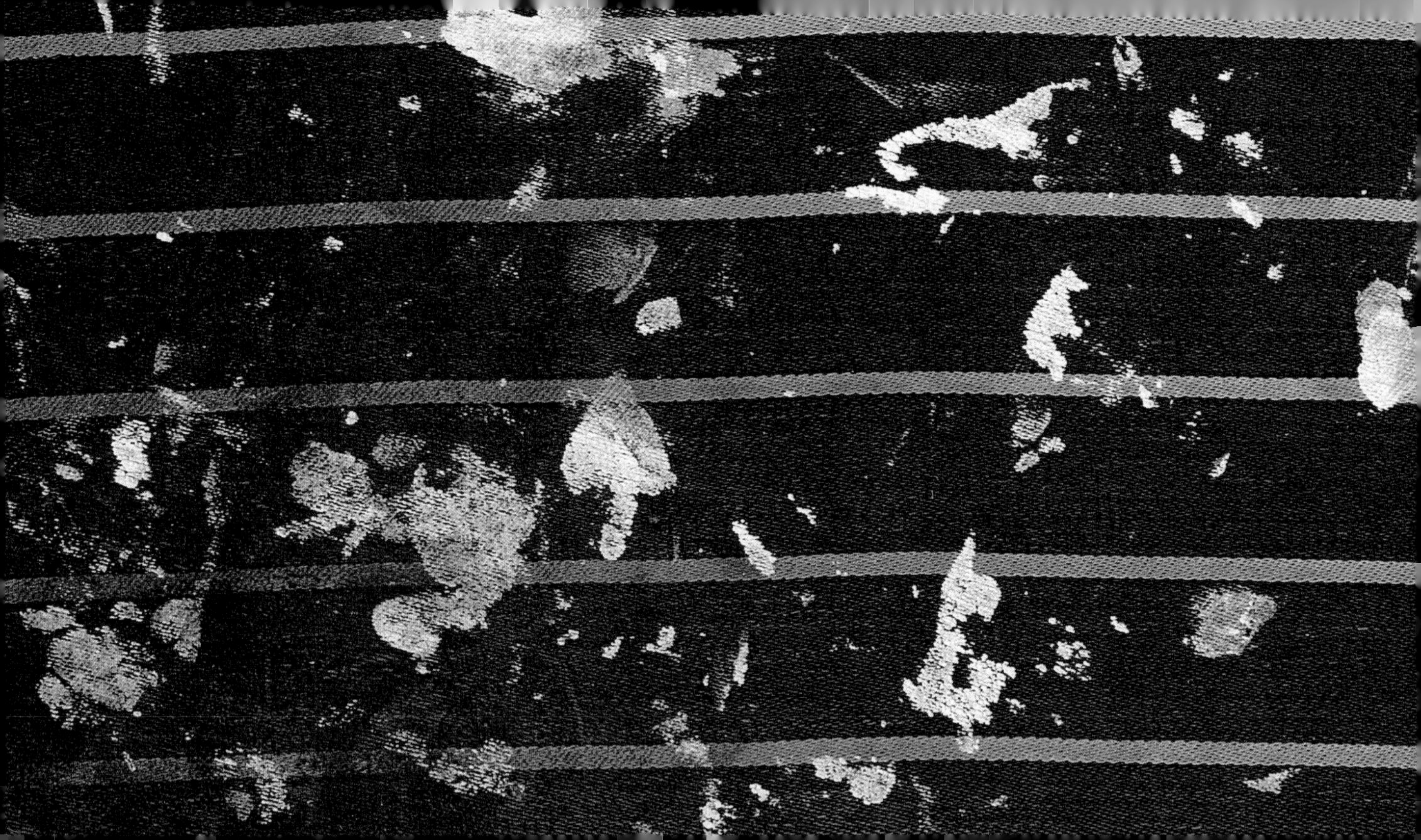

My mother makes things, too.

She has lots of colorful cloth, ribbons, lace, buttons, and thread.

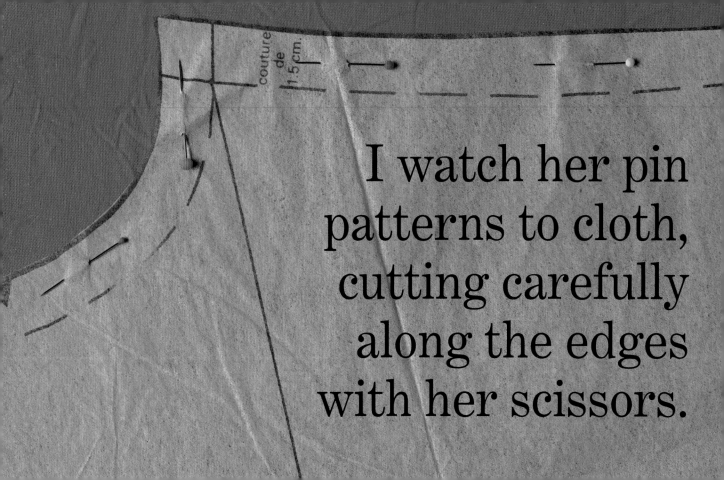

I watch her pin
patterns to cloth,
cutting carefully
along the edges
with her scissors.

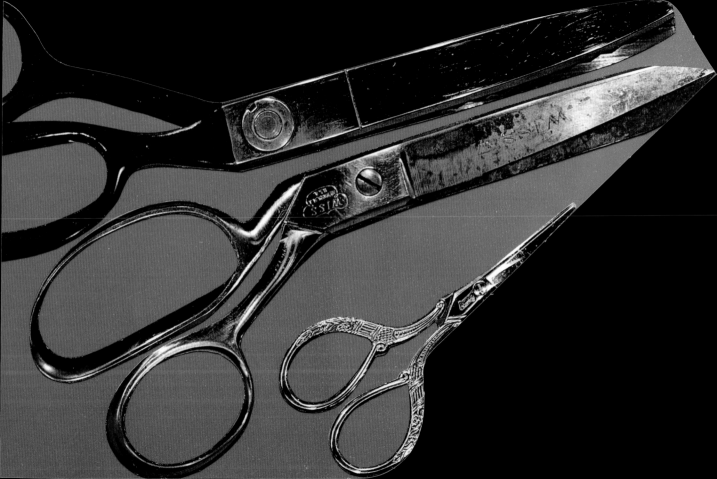

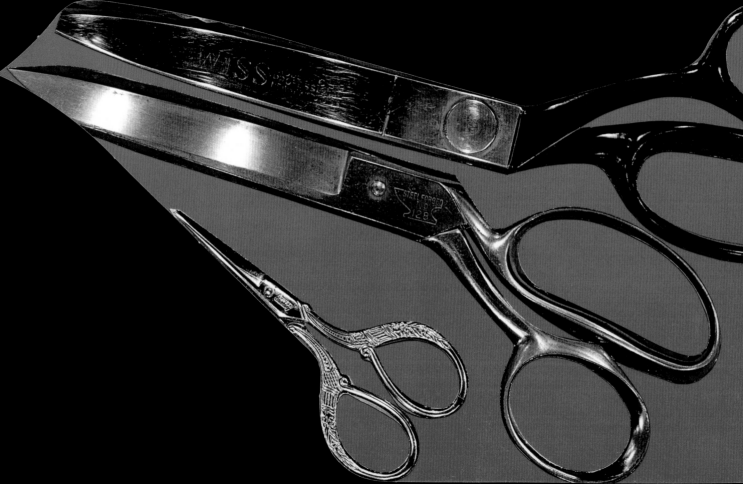

She has many scissors—
big, heavy ones and
pointy, little ones
that fit my hand.

She's teaching me to sew.

Together we make cat toys.

Today Dad put up a folding table near Mom's sewing machine. It's for me!

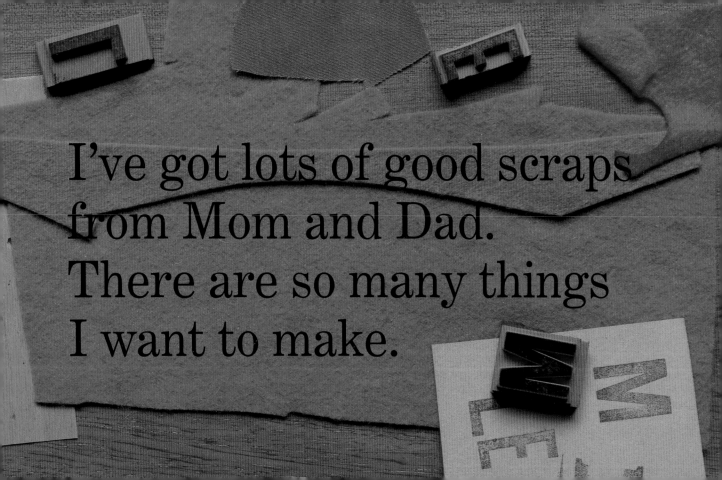

I've got lots of good scraps from Mom and Dad. There are so many things I want to make.

I just finished this pot holder for our kitchen.

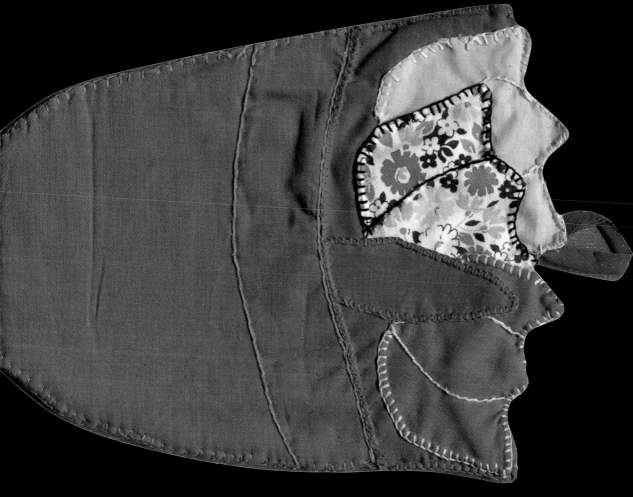

But I hear Dad calling me. They need extra hands in the garden.

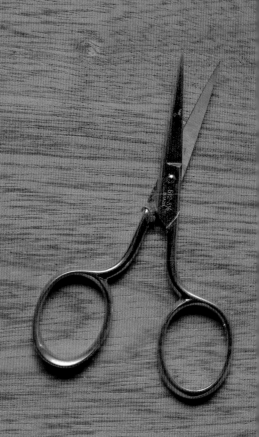

Every year
I help Dad plant
vegetable seeds.

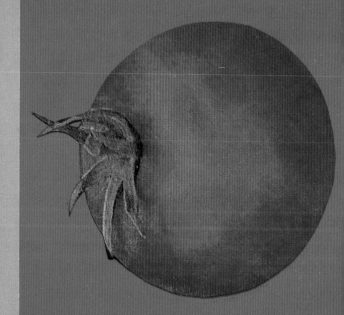

Early Red
TOMATO

HEARTLAND
SEED COMPANY

HEARTLAND
SEED COMPANY

Sun of Mexico
ZINNIA

Mom grows flowers.
She likes the
bright colors.
So do I.

I'm good at weeding.
Mom says I have
sharp eyes,
that I see things
other people miss.

When her
flowers bloom,
I'm going to paint
a picture of them.

I'll use every color
in my paint box.

Until then, I'll be working at my table, because I know, when I grow up,

I want
to be an
artist.

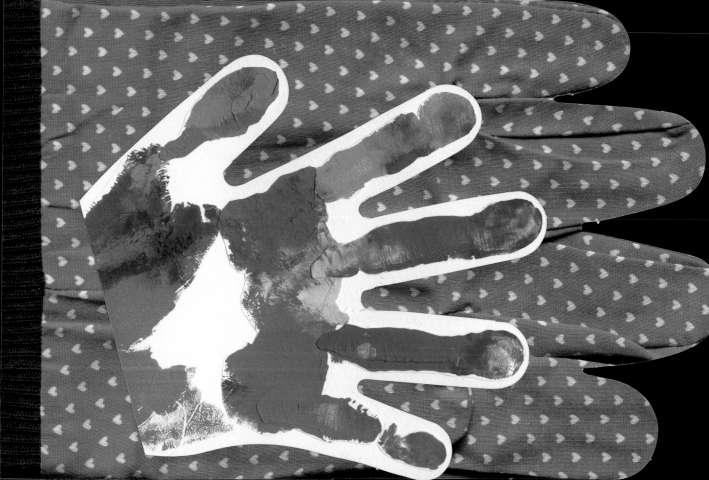

with my mom
and dad.